EVERYONE LOVES LUIGI...

"A FUNNY AND MOVING FANTASY. LUIGI IS EVERYMAN—MAYBE EVEN YOU!"
　　　　　　　　　　　　—Father Andrew Greeley

"THE CHARMING FAIRY TALE CHARACTERS, THE DESCRIPTIONS OF VENICE, THE WONDERFULLY PREPOSTEROUS PLOT TURNS—INDEED, ITS TONE—ALL SUGGEST THE SENSITIVE HAND OF A MASTER STORYTELLER."
　　　　　　　　　　　　—Digby Diehl

"WHERE *THE PRINCESS BRIDE* WAS LIGHTHEARTEDLY BRUTAL, THIS STORY IS GENTLY WHIMSICAL, WELL-COMPLEMENTED BY PAUL GIOVANOPOULOS' ZANY DRAWINGS."
　　　　　　　　　　　　—*San Francisco Examiner-Chronicle*

"THIS INVENTIVE, OFFBEAT FABLE HAS A TOUCH OF MAGIC ABOUT IT, AND HONORS THOSE WHO HOLD FAST TO DREAMS AGAINST GREAT ODDS."
　　　　　　　　　　　　—*Los Angeles Times*

...AND YOU WILL TOO!

William Goldman's

THE SILENT GONDOLIERS

A Fable by
S. MORGENSTERN
Author of *The Princess Bride*

Illustrated by Paul Giovanopoulos

A DEL REY BOOK

BALLANTINE BOOKS · NEW YORK

A Del Rey Book
Published by Ballantine Books

Copyright © 1983 by William Goldman

Library of Congress Catalog Card Number: 83-4631

ISBN 0-345-32583-4

Manufactured in the United States of America

First Hard Cover Editon: November 1983
First Paperback Edition: December 1985

Cover Art by Paul Giovanopoulos

TO URBAN DEL REY

Enclosed please find one copy of
The Silent Gondoliers.
*I am sending it first to you as my
American editor, because although I have
written in French and German as well as
Florinese, this is my initial attempt
at colloquial English.*

A request please. In your next edition of
The Princess Bride, *would you correct two
inaccuracies? The first is minor: you say my book
was written before* The Wizard of Oz. *This is
wrong—it was written before the movie,
not the Baum.*

*The second change is of more importance to me—
you say in several places that I am dead. As I
sit here and watch my fingers form this note,
I am forced to believe that you are in error.*

*I am old, but alive. Perhaps as you age, you
will find the two are not mutually exclusive.*

—S. Morgenstern

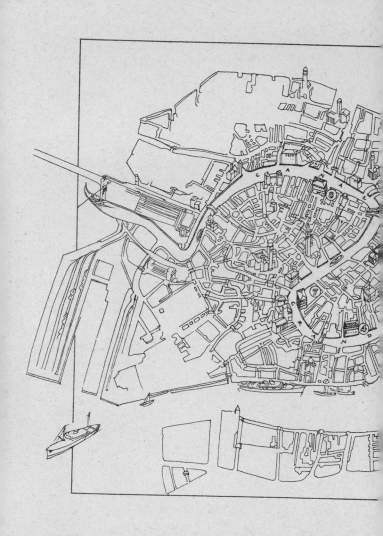

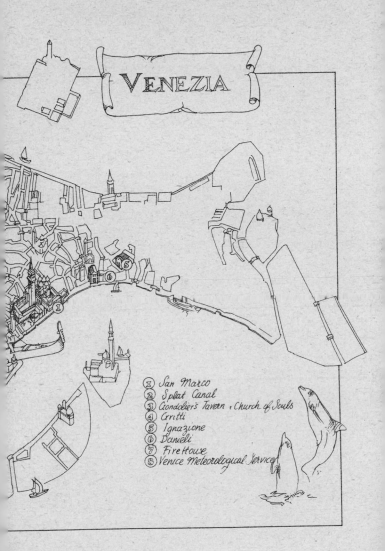

VENEZIA

1. San Marco
2. Splat Canal
3. Gondolier's Tavern & Church of Souls
4. Gritti
5. Ignazione
6. Danieli
7. Fire House
8. Venice Meteorological Service

The Silent Gondoliers

CHAPTER

I

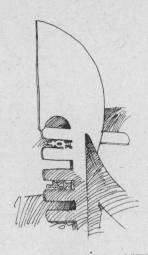

Everyone knows that the
gondoliers of Venice are
the greatest—

—correction, sorry—

—everyone *used to know* that the gondoliers of
Venice are the greatest singers in the world.

Probably you think that the above is ridiculous.
(I know I did when I began to research this
material.) After all, how can anybody be called
the "greatest" anything when there isn't any
accurate way to measure? It's possible to say that
I'm taller than you are; we can prove a statement
like that. We stand back to back and if my head is
above yours, I'm taller.

But if I say that Willie Mays is the "greatest"
baseball player of all time and you say, "Wrong,
Joe DiMaggio," there is no way of coming up with
an accurate answer. We can argue. I can point out
that Willie Mays hit more home runs and you say,

"So what, DiMaggio had a higher batting average," and we can go on like that for hours. Days. Might even be fun.

But in the end, nothing would be settled. I would know how stupid you were for not giving up on DiMaggio and you would be certain that I was a dummy for clinging to Willie.

Who is the greatest baseball player?

Obviously, a matter of opinion.

And who are the greatest singers?

Another matter of opinion?

Sorry.

I interviewed dozens of people, before I set this down, some of them in Venice, some in London, some in the United States. Singing experts, music historians, gondoliers, you name it. I have notebooks full of stuff I could bore you with, but I'll just give you two examples for proof. The first you can verify for yourself in any decent Almanac, the other is more personal.

The first example: The W.V.O.

The W.V.O. is not held anymore. Which is sad, of course, but what can you do? During its existence, it was the largest and most important musical event anywhere. In part that was because it took place only every four years. (W.V.O., in case any of you don't remember, stood for World Vocalizing Olympiad.)

The largest and most important of all the W.V.O.s was held in 1900. It was the beginning of a new century, there was a great spirit of optimism everywhere, and seven thousand four hundred and forty-seven singers gathered from fifty-two countries to compete for the twelve gold medals that year.

When it was done, the international panel of judges awarded *nine* of the *twelve* gold medals to Venetian gondoliers. Granted, that's impressive. (I mean, Venice is only a city of ninety thousand people and less than eight hundred of them had passed their Gondolier's Exam.)

What makes the result staggering is this: the other three golds were won by the Vizzini triplets of Rome—and they *had been* gondoliers, had spent all their lives on the canals until a death in the family forced them to move on to Rome in 1895.

If you don't think twelve out of twelve is proof of *something*, you are not only wrong, you are what my grandchildren would call weird . . .

The second example: Caruso.

Probably some of you knew about the 1900 W.V.O. results; as I said before, it's verifiable. (The Almanac I use lists them on Page 654—that's the 1982 edition, the one with the pink cover.)

I'm sure, though, that none of you knows the Caruso story, for reasons that will be clear in a couple of pages. It happened on Friday evening, the 11th of June, in Venice, on the Grand Canal, in the year 1903. I haven't been able to nail the time down precisely, but probably midnight would be close, give or take a few minutes one way or the other. Here's what happened.

Enrico Caruso (1873–1921) was, when he died, the most famous singer in the world. I think it's fair to say that even now, he is the most famous figure ever to have walked an opera or concert stage.

In 1903, he was a legend in Europe—but he had never sung in America. (He made his debut here in the fall of that year. And if you read his autobiography, it's clear he was very nervous about coming over.)

He had also never—and this is odd, since he was Italian—been to Venice. His one and only concert took place on the night of the story, at the La Fenice Theater, at eight o'clock, before an enthralled audience.

He was in superb voice and he sang for ninety minutes to a reaction that started with pandemonium and moved up from there. Twelve minutes of curtain calls, cheers and tears and a backstage party after.

Caruso was exhausted by this time, and he went to his hotel, the Danieli, and ordered room service to be sent up to his suite. The Danieli, proud of so famous a guest, saved his room service bill and I have a Xerox copy of it beside me now.

Caruso loved spaghetti and that is what he ordered. Spaghetti. With meat sauce. And another order with clam sauce. And a third with mushroom sauce. And he also had spaghetti carbonara and spaghetti with butter sauce and three other orders for which I can't make out the handwriting. (Enirco had a pretty good reputation as an eater.)

After dining he retired, but for reasons we don't know (I would have thought indigestion, but that's just a guess) he couldn't sleep.

At some minutes before midnight, he was seen, dressed casually now, walking through the lobby of his hotel and outside where the Danieli faces the Grand Canal.

The Grand Canal is the most glorious street in the world. Actually, it isn't a street at all but a waterway, winding through the heart of the city. Kind of in the shape of an inverted "S." Probably a hundred yards wide and close to two miles long. And it is flanked on both sides with a series of palaces. Over two hundred palaces, in fact, built in the course of six hundred years.

By day it is filled with boat traffic—water buses, delivery boats, gondolas—if something floats and it's in Venice, it moves along the Grand Canal. And by daylight it is one of the glories of the Earth.

But at night, especially when the moon is full and the soft illumination reflects off the water and onto the palaces— I don't know how to describe it so I won't, but if you died and in your will you asked for your ashes to be spread gently on the Grand Canal at midnight with a full moon, everyone would know this about you—you loved and understood beauty.

It was on just such a night (I've got the Venice weather report, another Xerox, right here, and the moon was officially and undeniably full) that Enrico Caruso stood staring at the Grand Canal. There was a single gondola moored in front of the Danieli, a small, shy middle-aged gondolier standing alongside. Caruso looked at the man and the boat for a moment, then took a step nearer.

"I assume you're free," Enrico Caruso said.

"Yessir," replied the shy gondolier.

> (*A note to the reader:*
>
> *Obviously, Caruso did not say, "I assume you're free." What he said was, "È libero?" The reason he put it that way was because at this time in his life, he only spoke Italian. What I've done all through this is put the foreign dialog into kind of colloquial English. I've done the same with the names too—because I find most of their words hard for American audiences to*

*grasp quickly—all the names, I should add,
except of course, Luigi.*

*There may someday be an Italian version of
this, in which case, I won't include this reader's
note. I only put it in here to show I know that
from a scholarly point of view, what I'm doing
isn't proper. I suppose I'm trying to reach a
wider audience. In any case, for you professors
and critics who might see this, I'm aware of the
changes, and also that they're not strictly kosher,
but there it is.)*

"I assume you're free."

"Yessir."

"How much?"

*(Another note to the reader, a quickie, I
promise.*

*Even though Caruso asked about price, I don't
want anyone thinking bad thoughts about him,
such as that he was money hungry. And "How
much" seems kind of rude.*

*The fact is, for all their good points, gondoliers
are tough with a buck. Last year's Venice
Tourist Report shows that 85 percent of the
tourists who were questioned got zapped by
gondoliers when it came to paying them. Swiss
bankers are softies compared to gondoliers.*

*Caruso was not being rude by getting right
down to cases. He was just forestalling a
screaming match later.)*

"I assume you're free."

"Yessir."

"How much?"

"For you? Nothing."

"I haven't told you how long a ride I wanted."

"If you wanted to travel across the seven seas, the price would still be the same."

Caruso took a step toward the boat when the shy gondolier came quickly toward him, held out an arm to guide the great singer toward the cushioned seat.

"I'm not old yet," Caruso said. "I can get in by myself quite handily."

The shy gondolier kept his arm out. "I'm afraid you might change your mind. Having you as a passenger will be the high point of my life."

Caruso allowed the gondolier to help him into the boat.

"Would you like another pillow? Anything at all."

"I'm quite comfortable."

The gondolier moved to the rope that attached his boat to the small wooden pier, deftly freed the craft, took his pole and pushed off.

"I want to see the Grand Canal by moonlight."

"My delight to serve you."

They started on their journey.

Palace after palace slid silently by; Gothic and Byzantine, Lombard and Baroque. The great water street was quiet, just a few other gondolas and an occasional fisherman, rowing exhausted home.

"How did you know who I was?" Caruso asked.

"How could I not," the shy gondolier answered quietly from behind him at the rear of the boat, where he stood, smoothly working his single oar.

"Did you hear my concert?"

"I am a poor working man; I could not afford a seat. Only the mighty were inside tonight. What a triumph for you."

"They only cried and cheered for twelve minutes," Caruso said. "I wasn't sure they liked me."

"They adored you. I listened outside the theater for hours. I could not hear you, of course, but it was enough knowing you were there. When it was done, I watched their faces when they left. Their eyes sparkled."

"Did you hear what they said?"

"I could not avoid hearing some comments. 'Fantastic.' 'Phenomenal.' 'Legendary.'"

"That was all?" Caruso asked. "Nothing more positive?"

"Many were still weeping," the gondolier explained.

"That explains it," Caruso said. "My true fans must have been still too overcome to speak."

The gondola continued its magical journey.

"Were there more 'legendaries' or 'phenomenals'?" Caruso asked then.

"'Legendary' ten to one. And but a single 'fantastic.'"

"That's some consolation," Caruso allowed. He looked back at the small gondolier. "You stood outside the whole concert?"

"From a half hour before until half an hour afterward. I wanted to spend more time, but I had to earn some money tonight."

"You must be a music lover."

The shy gondolier nodded.

"And do you sing?"

"I'm a gondolier, so I must."

Caruso put his hands behind his head and stretched out in the boat. "Sing for me then," Caruso said.

"I would not dare."

"I ask you again. It would be a nice change to have someone else do the entertaining."

"It would humiliate me, please," the shy gondolier said.

"Do you know the words to *O Sole Mio?*"

The gondolier, his hands shaking on his oar now, finally nodded.

"Sing."

The shy gondolier shook his head.

"I am not asking, you are here to serve me, I am *commanding* you to sing."

The shy gondolier stood frozen.

"It begins this way, and I'm starting to lose my patience. Just copy me," and Caruso hummed the famous opening notes of the song. He turned and glared at the boatman.

Under the pressure of the famous face, the gondolier opened his mouth and started—except his throat was so dry from panic that all that came out was a croak.

"Moisten your throat and try again," Caruso ordered.

This time the gondolier managed a whisper.

"I'm truly getting annoyed," Caruso said. "It's so easy. All you do is just take a breath and, if God has blessed you with genius, this is what it sounds like—"

And for the first time, the most famous voice

in history echoed across the stone palaces of the Grand Canal. Caruso sang the opening few lines, pleased as the echo caressed his ears—truly he had never sounded better. He closed his eyes, stopped singing—

—only the echo went on . . .

Caruso spun around and stared back.

The shy gondolier was the only one singing now.

"My God," Caruso began.

"Forgive me, am I displeasing you? Am I still too soft for you, too low, I'll do my best," the shy gondolier said, and his voice rose half an octave, doubled in power—

—and in purity.

Caruso still stared.

Panicked now, the shy gondolier, so afraid of disapproval, went up half an octave and doubled his power again—

—and doubled his purity too.

The stone palaces listened.

"Stop!" Caruso cried.

"I'm sorry, I'm sorry, I've offended," the shy gondolier said, and he turned his blushing face away, stared down at his oar.

Finally, Caruso was able to say, "You must be the greatest singing gondolier in the world—"

—and now there was laughter.

Caruso spun again to face the sound. From both sides of the boat it came—he looked left, right, left again—

Half a dozen gondoliers were rowing their empty crafts along the canal.

"The greatest?" one of them managed.

"*The greatest?* He is ranked fifty-third. And lucky to be that high." (The gondoliers have their own annual contest and judge themselves. They are not easy on each other.)

And now another voice started to sing, so high and pure it put the shy gondolier's to shame. "I am rated thirty-fifth," the voice sang.

From the other side of the boat, a more perfect vocal sound yet. "And I am twenty-second."

"And I am eleventh."

"And I, ninth."

"Sixth, but with hopes of improvement."

And now, finally, the greatest vocalist of all, George of the Gritti, in perfect form—"This is what the greatest singing gondolier sounds like" and, and—

—and it was at this point that Caruso clasped both hands over his ears and stared wild-eyed as the laughing men sang their rankings louder and louder, their boats coming closer—

—and it was at *this* point that Caruso, able to take no more, dove from the gondola into the Grand Canal and swam madly toward the water's edge. Why he did this no one can be certain— perhaps he thought he was caught up in a nightmare.

But when he at last staggered into the entrance of the Danieli Hotel, he was still very wet indeed. (The night concierge made a note of the event. I have the Xerox by me now.) Caruso spoke to no one, fled to his room, and left Venice by dawn's light the following morning, never ever to return.

.　　.　　.

Enough of proof; time to get to Luigi.

But I must add one final jot—when I said at the start that the gondoliers of Venice are the greatest singers in the world, that was not strictly true—

—because, as everyone knows, the gondoliers don't sing anymore.

Oh, if you're in Venice and you want music for a gondola ride, they'll get you music, by hustling up some old accordion player or the like.

But they themselves, the gondoliers, are silent now.

What follows is as accurate an explanation of that mysterious silence as several months of scholarly research has enabled me to find . . .

II

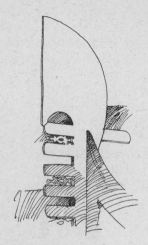

But how accurate, in truth, is what follows?

The answer, again in truth, is I can't be sure. Gondoliers are notoriously close-mouthed private people. At the same time, they are notoriously contemptuous of facts.

From a researcher's point of view, their characteristics do present something of a problem. You strike up a conversation with a gondolier—and he ignores you. You try again, explaining who you are and what you want—and he turns his back. You persist—he goes for espresso. You accompany him, pay for him—he grunts what might be "thank you" and returns to his boat.

This can go on, let me assure you, for days.

Until at last, usually without warning, his words come tumbling out. You scribble frantically (I developed a kind of shorthand for this project) and he notices your effort, speaks even faster. On and on he goes until at last, again usually without warning, silence.

Back you hurry to your room, transcribe what he's told you—and when you do that you realize there may not be a speck of reality in what you hold in your hand. Back you go to the boatman—only to find he is in his silent mood again. You say, "Let me check one or two things with you." (Say, for example, his memories of the Killer Storm. It is still referred to as that, even now, in Venice—the "Killer Storm.") You read what he's told you. He listens. Then he says, "Interesting stuff, where did you get it? Not from me, certainly." And then he is off for another espresso.

Not easy subjects, the gondoliers.

But I had time. I'm old now, or at least that's what my eyes tell me when they greet my face in the morning mirror; a lifelong writer of books, whose thoughts tend occasionally to wander, which is what they're doing now—

—back to the subject at hand, that being accuracy. Or, to be more precise, why my desperate need for accuracy.

Simply put: As a child, I heard the gondoliers sing.

A brightening Christmas morning it was. I suppose I was five or six and like most children, awake early on that children's day. And at dawn, waiting for my parents to rise, my room was invaded by the glory of their song—I ran to my window which overlooked one of the small canals and a group of gondoliers were rowing their way. Such was the glass-like purity of their sound I forgot Santa Claus until they had rounded a corner, heading toward the Grand Canal.

Why was I in Venice on a Christmas morning?

My last name is Morgenstern, clearly not one of Italian origin. My father, upon completion of his medical studies, scandalized his family by impulsively declaring that being a pill peddler did nothing for the soul—so he was off to Venice to become an artist.

How skilled he might have been we will never know, because on his second day in the city, he saw a young Italian girl crossing the Piazza San Marco and was, so Morgenstern family legend has it, smitten on sight. The girl was going to the Danieli Hotel, where her father Frank (Francesco) had his station.

Frank worked, as his family had for generations, at the Danieli, as a gondolier. In point of fact, the shy man who took Caruso on his midnight ride was my mother's father, which is how that story came to me—and why I vouch for its truth. I never knew my grandfather well, but he was noted for his honesty and humility and when he got home after the Caruso trip, he was so shaken by what had transpired he poured it all out in detail to my grandmother, who wrote down what he told her.

I'm digressing again, wandering again—the point is my father followed my mother the rest of that day, finally got the courage to speak, and within a week they were engaged and he was making plans to get quickly home and hang out his shingle. Without regret. To be a starving artist only has glamour if you have no family to support.

We visited Venice often after I was born, which is a long way of explaining how I happened, by chance, to hear the Christmas gondoliers.

Now I must jump half a century and more. This past Christmas, with my family wonderfully around me, my wife and daughters (two) and grandchildren (four and a half), I went to sleep early. Dozed off in my rocker.

And woke, startled—

—because in my dream I heard the sound again of the Christmas gondoliers. And as I blinked I realized that no child today is privileged to hear such glory.

And what a terrible thing that was.

I was instantly obsessed—why did they sing no more? What was the reason? Why was the world so deprived?

I left for Venice within a week and did my research and, of course, what follows is the answer. Except now, knowing what I know, I don't imagine that their silence is a terrible thing at all.

How can the removal of beauty from a world so lacking in beauty be anything but tragic?

That is what follows.

And can the loss of beauty be anything but bad?

That is for you to decide . . .

III

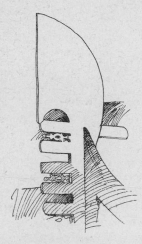

Until his first day at Gondoliers' School, nobody knew that Luigi was anything out of the ordinary.

The reason nobody knew he was anything out out of the ordinary was this: nobody really knew Luigi at all. Oh, he was popular enough. He was eighteen and slender and taller than most, with black hair and eyes. He would have been handsome except he had this smile the Italians called *"tontone"* which is hard to translate—there is no exact equivalent in English. The closest I can come is this: "goony." He had a goony smile. He was strong but very gentle, and no one could ever remember his having done a mean thing since he was five and, in truth, it couldn't have been *that* mean, since no one could remember what exactly he did back then. "Oh yes," his mother would say; "Luigi has a fine disposition and except for once when he was five, I have no complaints." When pressured as to what he had done she said, "Oh, something, you know how boys are."

Gondoliers' School deals strictly with seamanship, and it is a three-year course. That's the minimum. Some young men take five or even six years to get their Gondolier's Diploma. The school is run by a small staff, all retired gondoliers, and it is an honor to be a teacher. The only requirement to be on the staff is this: you must not just be a retired gondolier (preferably with thirty-five years or more of service), you must also be bad tempered. Only the cruelest qualify for teaching positions.

The reason is this: it is extraordinarily difficult to make a gondola go smoothly, and only experts get diplomas. If you had a sweet-natured fellow running the operation, he might pass a young man who wasn't good enough and once word got out that there was an incompetent gondolier working the Grand Canal, rumors would surely spread that the caliber of gondoliers was down. The reason the rumor would surely spread is this: everyone in Venice is jealous of the gondoliers. It is the finest job in the city if not all Europe, and the highest standards must be upheld at all times.

The reason it is difficult to make a gondola run smoothly is that the gondola is a weird-looking boat. It is very long—twenty-five feet—and very heavy—thirteen hundred pounds. It is also shaped like the bottom of a coffee saucer, like a mild "U." The shape is necessary because the gondolier stands on the back of the boat and steers with his single oar, and if the gondola were shaped, say, like a canoe, the minute the gondolier stood on the back his weight would make the boat capsize.

There are many tests along the way during the three years, but for centuries, there has only been one final exam—"*Tombolon* Corner." Again, there is no exact equivalent for "*Tombolon*"—the closest I can come, I am embarrassed to say, is this: "SPLAT." SPLAT Corner is the final exam.

SPLAT Corner got its name because so many gondolas go SPLAT when they try and navigate it. It is in a very out-of-the-way part of Venice, one, in fact, that few natives even know about. The two narrowest canals in Venice intersect, and the total turning space has been measured exactly at seven feet eight inches.

To take a twenty-five-foot boat and make it turn a corner seven feet eight inches wide is not the easiest thing in the world to do.

On the first day of Gondoliers' School, in order to frighten the students, the cruelest teacher available takes all the young men and says, "Follow me." The students don't know where they are going, but after an hour's trip, the teacher suddenly stops, points, and says, "That, you miserable idiots, is your final exam."

One-third of each class, on the average, decides then and there to seek some other form of occupation.

On Luigi's first day, Luigi and the four other would-be gondoliers took the trek to SPLAT Corner and the teacher stopped and pointed dramatically and said, "Look, you peanut-brained imbeciles, look at your final exam."

Two of the class decided immediately to open souvenir stands in the Piazza San Marco and left without a word. A third turned deadly pale. The fourth, the one nearest Luigi, began trembling

out of control as he repeated the word,
"Impossible, impossible," again and again.

To try and make the poor fellow feel better,
Luigi whispered, "Perhaps he's just trying to
frighten us, it can't be that difficult."

Unfortunately, sound travels over water and
they were standing by the waters of the canal.
The teacher that day happened to be John the
Bastard, by far the cruelest man ever to grace the
board of directors of the Gondoliers' School.

"*Luigi*," he snapped.

Now Luigi turned deadly pale.

"Not so hard, eh?" said John the Bastard. "I
heard you and I'm not surprised—you've got a bad
reputation—everyone knows you did something
mean when you were five."

"I was only trying—" Luigi began. "I was only
trying to make him feel better" was what he meant
to say. But John the Bastard hollered "Silence!"

Luigi stopped his thought.

"You think we're jokes at Gondoliers' School,
isn't that right, Luigi? You think SPLAT Corner
is easy, isn't that so, Luigi?" He stood directly in
front of Luigi now, and he bellowed: "Well, we'll
just see. All of you stay right here."

He left them at attention and when he came
back, he was rowing his own personal gondola.
All black (gondolas are black—by law) and shiny.
He got out and gestured for Luigi to get in.
"See how easy it is, smart guy—"

Luigi didn't understand and said so.

"I want you to make the turn at SPLAT
Corner," John the Bastard said. "If it's not so
hard—that's what you said, I'm just quoting you—
you should be able to do it without scratching my

gondola." And now he made a horrible smile.
"And if you do scratch it—even a tiny mark so
small that the eye can't see—your punishment will
be to shine my gondola every night after class for
the next three years. Or five years. Or however long
it takes you to graduate, and since I'm your
teacher I can promise you I don't think you'll
ever graduate."

Luigi gulped and stood alone in John the
Bastard's boat, holding the oar. He looked at
SPLAT Corner, all of seven feet eight inches at its
widest point. He looked at the gondola, all of
twenty-five feet in length. Then he closed his eyes
and shook his head.

(I should add at this point that the normal
training procedure at Gondoliers' School is this:
you don't even think about attempting SPLAT
Corner until midway through the second year. Then
you begin with a little boat the size of a bathtub.
Then, when you've mastered that, you get a slightly
bigger bathtub. Then a rowboat. Then a bigger
rowboat. Then a small canoe, a large canoe, etc.
Even with all this training, only three candidates
in this century have made the SPLAT Corner turn
the first time without severely damaging their
gondolas.)

"*Go!*" John the Bastard shouted.

Luigi kind of zipped around SPLAT Corner and
out of sight with a foot of clearance on each side.

John the Bastard's immediate instinct was to
flee to the famous Gondolier's Tavern and have a
gallon of beer to settle his nerves. But his reputation
for toughness was well earned, and he managed
to shout "*Blind Luck!*"

Luigi, out of sight around the corner, spoke

very loudly. "I couldn't quite make out what you said."

"I said come back here!" John the Bastard cried.

Luigi returned through SPLAT Corner—only there wasn't room to turn the boat totally around so this time he did it backwards.

At the sight of his gondola coming toward him in reverse, John the Bastard sort of came unglued. He muttered and sputtered and spittle came to his lips and he blinked his eyes and shook his head before managing to get out, "Two gallons of beer, *at least* two gallons of beer." Then he turned and raced off in the direction of the Gondolier's Tavern.

Class was definitely over for the day.

How did Luigi manage such an extraordinary feat? For Luigi, it wasn't extraordinary at all. Remember I mentioned before that no one knew him well? The reason for that was this: Luigi had secrets.

He had known all his life he would someday be a gondolier; his family had been in that occupation for hundreds of years. And he loved his father's boat. Nothing pleased him more than sitting and watching the palaces go by as his father rowed smoothly with the single oar.

Luigi never needed much sleep and when he was seven or eight, he used to get up before dawn and creep out and sit in his father's gondola and imagine great voyages. These imaginings grew as he did, and when he was thirteen, he first had the courage to take the boat for little rides by himself. While the rest of Venice slept.

By the time he was fifteen his little rides grew longer, and one day he became so absorbed that he realized too late that the sun was soon to rise.

He knew he could never get home undiscovered unless he tried some shortcuts.

One of those shortcuts was SPLAT Corner.

Luigi didn't know its name then. All he knew was that he'd found this terrific narrow place for cutting the time home in half, and so great was his fear of his father's discovering what he'd done, he just went through it without much thought.

From then on, he always took the shortcut. For five years he'd been rowing in semi-darkness along the back canals, always getting safely home in time, tying up the boat, scooting up to bed before anyone suspected.

The fact that what he had done was fairly unusual was something he never realized until that first, soon to be famous, day in class. (There was talk of nothing else in the Gondolier's Tavern for weeks. At one point it was suggested to pass Luigi then and there—since it was obvious you couldn't teach him anything about the gondola, why try and teach him about the gondola? But ultimately the decision was to have him stay the full three years. No one had ever graduated in less, and gondoliers love tradition.)

As I said, Luigi had secrets. This, the dark silent pre-dawn rides, was a little secret. Luigi, like the rest of us, had lots of little secrets.

He also had his one Great Secret. Which we will come to shortly. It was his Great Secret that ultimately broke his heart . . .

IV

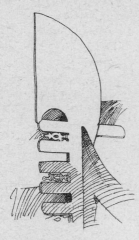

The day after he graduated from Gondoliers' School Luigi went to work. His first jobs were to become even more famous than his now legendary navigation of SPLAT Corner.

There was a great deal of pressure on him.

A gondolier's family keeps the same location on the Grand Canal generation after generation. And Luigi's spot was the same as that of his great-great-grandfather—and not a prime location either.

Luigi's family's mooring spot was in front of probably the worst hotel on the entire canal, the Ignazione. Not the Danieli or the Gritti Palace or any of the other splendid places. The reason was simple: no one in Luigi's family tree had been a particularly outstanding gondolier. They got by, but just.

Luigi was to change all that—and that was the reason for some of the pressure. The rest was

supplied by his mother and his six sisters, who stood
in front of the hotel, watching and waiting for
Luigi's very first fare. His father was moored in
the next gondola, eating nibbles of Gorgonzola
cheese. (He hated Gorgonzola cheese but when he
was nervous, nothing else soothed his stomach
as well.)

And of course, Laura was watching too.

Laura Lorenzini was twenty and by far the most
beautiful girl in all Venice. She had green eyes and
night-black hair that tumbled down to her fanny.
The Venice town council had, the previous year,
contemplated ruling her figure illegal, such were the
thoughts it put in the minds of old men. She worked
in a small grocery store that belonged to her father.
She dreamed of but one thing: marrying a
gondolier. A great gondolier. A gondolier so
talented he might be able to do SPLAT Corner
without trembling.

She and Luigi had known each other always.
But they had never spoken a great deal because she
was so beautiful and always pursued by handsome
men. Besides who was he, a would-be gondolier,
poor, with nothing much to offer out of the
ordinary except his goony smile.

At the end of his first week in Gondoliers'
School, Luigi was walking home when Laura
moved into his path and they bumped.

Embarrassed at his clumsiness, Luigi could
barely apologize—and when he did, his face was so
scarlet he turned away and hurried home.

The next day they bumped again, and this time
her handkerchief fell. He retrieved it, shoved it
into her hands and ran away, redder than the day
before. "Why didn't you talk to her?" he scolded

himself. "If you had said something she might have said something back—you might have actually had a conversation with Laura Lorenzini. Maybe she likes goony smiles. Maybe you could have taken her for a gondola ride. In the moonlight. Maybe suddenly it would get cold. She might have forgotten to wear a shawl. What if she shivered? You could have offered her your arms to keep warm—

—you could have held Laura Lorenzini in your arms!

Luigi slept less than usual that night. For he had loved her since the third grade when she had beaten him at rocks (Venetian children are not allowed to play marbles—in point of fact, marbles, balls and most hard round things are illegal there—because supposing a tourist tripped on a marble and broke a hip and that got in the newspapers and people began thinking the place wasn't safe. The only round things Venetian children can play with are balloons, the town council having ruled that if a tourist is stupid enough to trip on a balloon, he deserves what he gets.)

He had loved her, and now he had lost her forever. They never would bump each other again.

And they didn't.

The next day, when they were about to bump she pulled up short and handed him a dead squid. "We were having a special at Pop's store and no one bought this one. Here, I remember in school you were always big on squid."

Now Luigi, if anything, was always small on squid. They tasted rubbery and even little ones didn't thrill him to look at. But this one he clutched in both hands and said, "Oh, what a treat, I haven't had a squid to eat since breakfast."

He was about to go on about his mother's various squid recipes when he could tell he was going all scarlet again, so he spun away. And home he went, angry, of course, at his cursed shyness, but also amazed at the little accidents life plays. Here he had gone months and months without so much as a glimpse of night-black Laura and then, amazingly, the first week of Gondoliers' School, they had met three times.

That night, Luigi did some heavy thinking.

A girl and a boy bump—surely an accident.

A girl and a boy bump and her handkerchief drops—surely another accident.

But when a girl gives a boy a dead squid—*that had to mean something*.

What, though?

Luigi tussled with that one all night. Because the answer he kept coming up with was impossible —that answer being, of course, that she was maybe, possibly, just conceivably, at least for a little while, interested in him.

I think I might give my life for that, Luigi thought.

It turned out he didn't have to—it turned out she was. She gave him a handful of macaroni salad the next day, and his face reddened only a little.

Later that month, he took her for a gondola ride. It was hot and they both were sweating, but he put his arms around her anyway. And whether she kissed him first or the other way around, neither was ever really sure. But she was sure of one thing: her love was greater than his.

They became engaged, had been for two years and were to marry as soon as he was successfully established as a great gondolier, by Christmas if possible.

This was now June, June the first, and Luigi waited in front of the Ignazione, trying to ignore his father stuffing down the Gorgonzola, trying to ignore his mother and his six sisters, who giggled and waved at him, trying to not think of Laura, watching him so proudly, perfect Laura with her night-black hair.

At precisely 10:06 A.M., the Gretchner family of Baltimore, Maryland exited the Ignazione and moved toward the waiting gondoliers. There was Mr. Gretchner, who tended to be quiet, which was why he was not a very successful life insurance salesman. There was Punky Gretchner, who was nine and a terror. There was Binky Gretchner, who whined and hated her one-year-older brother. And there was Mrs. Gretchner, who weighed 200 pounds and ran things.

Mrs. Gretchner pulled out her Berlitz book and stomped up to Luigi's father. "*Vorrei shampoo e messa in piega,*" she said, which confused the Gorgonzola eater, since "*Vorrei shampoo e messa in piega*" means "I want a shampoo and set" in Italian.

"Perhaps you're on the wrong page," Luigi suggested, in his very best English. He didn't speak English very well, but in Gondoliers' School they do prepare you for people asking weird things from their Berlitz books.

Mrs. Gretchner turned back a page from Hairdressers to Gondoliers, and she and Luigi quickly struck a deal. He gallantly helped Binky

34

and Punky and the elder Gretchners into his boat, and, sneaking a quick smile to his beloved Laura Lorenzini, he untied his gondola and pushed off into the Grand Canal.

"I'm getting seasick," Binky Gretchner said then.

"You make *me* sick," Punky Gretchner countered, proud of his rhyme.

"*Children*," Mr. Gretchner managed. It was the main part of his vocabulary when dealing with his off-spring.

Mrs. Gretchner then turned, Berlitz book in hand, and said, "*Desidero un francobollo per questa cartolina*," which means, "I'd like a stamp for my postcard." But Luigi, fresh from his gondolier's training, knew what she meant and answered, "My name is Luigi, madam." (This was very thoughtful and bright of Luigi, no question, but it somewhat damaged the rest of the Gretchner's Venice visit, since every time she met other Venetians and asked them what they were called, most looked confused and pointed toward the nearest post office.)

"Sing for us, Luigi," Mrs. Gretchner said. "Do you know *O Sole Mio*? If you do, sing it for us now."

The time was 10:17.

And Luigi began to sing.

And no one knew it then, of course, but history was about to be made.

"*O SOLE MIO*," Luigi started

Binky screamed and Bunky groaned and Mr. Gretchner turned pale and Mrs. Gretchner put her hands to her temples and—

"*O SOLE MIO*," Luigi repeated.

By now the Gretchner monsters were clinging

The Gretchner Family

Baltimore Maryland

U.S.A.

together and Mr. Gretchner was gripping the sides of the gondola and no one knows what would have happened next if Mrs. Gretchner had not cried out, at the very top of her very considerable voice, *"STOPPPP . . ."*

Luigi, of course, did as he was told. For a moment, there was silence in the gondola.

(During that silence I think it best if I add here a note or two of research. I spoke to a grandchild of the Gretchner family—not easy to locate, but I am dogged, a terrier by nature—and the Venice trip had assumed something of legendary status within the clan. Apparently, what Binky and Punky mostly remembered was endless walking toward various post offices. But the vocal moment on the canal was not easily forgotten. Either Binky or Punky thought the gondolier was angry and was going to kill them and the other one thought his (or her) head was going to pop.

So much for the Gretchner's memories.

I also interviewed many vocal experts, some of whom were Italian; and, of course, there are no records of Luigi's voice so what follows is conjecture.

Clearly, Luigi was tone deaf.

He had no idea if he was singing one note higher or lower than the one preceding. But that alone is not enough to explain the reaction that transpired after his attempts at vocalizing.

Luigi also had a voice of extraordinary power.

*Coupled with a total lack of pitch and a
blasting quality, Luigi possessed an all but
unique sound. When he lifted his voice in song,
the listener did not so much want to faint as
he wanted to get away. When Luigi sang, you got
an instant headache. There are medical reasons
I could go into, but no point. Facts are facts.
In today's media-oriented age, the Bayer Aspirin
people probably would have put Luigi under
contract and used him in television commercials.*

*But this, of course, was long ago. The silence
is over—back to the Gretchners.)*

"Just row," Mrs. Gretchner commanded.
Luigi just rowed.

Then Mr. Gretchner said, "I didn't pay for a
rowing gondolier, I can get rowed back in
Baltimore."

"Shall we ask him to try again?" Mrs.
Gretchner asked.

She meant to say more, but then Binky and
Punky, still clinging to each other, cried, "No,
mommy, no, we'll be good, we promise, we'll be
so good, don't let him do it again."

Mrs. Gretchner turned and scowled at Luigi,
pointing toward the Ignazione Hotel, not far away.
"Back!" she commanded.

At 10:24, Luigi's first trip was ignominiously
over. It had taken a total of eighteen minutes. No
one could have dreamed that this would be the
high point of his professional singing life as a
gondolier.

The second trip—it began at 11:11—actually took longer than the first. Half an hour on the dot. (This was because they had gone a bit further along the Grand Canal before the passengers—two elderly schoolteachers from Des Moines— requested *O Sole Mio*.) But the younger of the teachers—she was sixty-two—who admittedly was feeling poorly to begin with, got a migraine headache and her companion complained to the management of the Ignazione Hotel.

It was on the third trip that people first started throwing fish at Luigi.

He was tooling along the Grand Canal, belting away, when a flounder was hurled from one of the palace windows in order to silence him. The flounder, it should be noted, missed, though it did make a considerable splash alongside his gondola.

The next fish—a few seconds later—also missed Luigi, though it did strike a glancing blow to one of his three passengers, a German businessman.

Then came a rain of smelt—windows were opening in all the palaces now, and all kinds of objects were pitched toward Luigi's gondola, anything to stifle the sound. Luigi, always game, kept on singing until another of the German businessmen said to his fellows, "*Gott in Himmel? Von welches Dreck . . . ?*" which, roughly translated, means, "Hey, what is this shit?"

Since the businessmen agreed they did not come to Venice to get garbaged, they angrily returned to the Ignazione and voiced some very loud complaints.

The management was keeping a very close eye on Luigi by this time.

His fourth trip—his last solo journey as it turned out—was also his briefest. A sweet music-loving French woman asked Luigi to sing as she stepped into his boat.

She was still standing as he began, and perhaps her balance wasn't the best, no one can say with certainty. But she did fall into the canal and, as it turned out, could not swim. Luigi gallantly rescued her, diving in immediately, and he deposited her with profuse apologies on the dock—

But the hotel owners had witnessed the event and immediately conferred with Luigi's humiliated father. Luigi was, they told him, finished working in front of the Ignazione. Luigi's father protested that his family had been there for past generations. The hotel management replied that they had their eye on *future* generations, and sick and wet customers didn't do a lot for word of mouth. Luigi's father threatened all kinds of action—he would take his own gondola to another hotel, etc., etc.—but the threats were hollow. No major hotel would have him and clearly someone in the family had to make a living.

Finally he went to his son, who had stood there watching the discussion and trying very hard to keep his goony smile on, and muttered, "Maybe you better go home, we'll talk over dinner."

Luigi rowed his gondola home.

Dinner was not a happy event that night. Luigi's six sisters had been taunted in school during afternoon recess, and they stayed up in their rooms. His mother, who had wept the day away, stood sniffling by the stove. Laura Lorenzini, wondrous Laura with the night-black hair, picked at her food. Luigi's father, who was a bit tipsy

from his normal after-work stop at the Gondolier's Tavern, tried to put the best possible light on the situation.

"Maybe you could sing softer," he suggested.

"I *was* singing softer," Luigi told him. "I was afraid to go full out."

"And a good thing too," his mother sniffled from the stove. "You might have killed somebody."

"I never knew you sang that way," his father said.

"*I* did," Luigi told him. "Why do you think I've only hummed since I was little? And I only do that when I'm sure I'm alone."

Laura stared down at her plate.

"Maybe I could specialize in passengers who just want to ride in a gondola," Luigi managed.

"Nobody wants just to *ride* in a gondola," his father said. "They want to be *entertained* in a gondola. They want music, Luigi. They want glorious songs."

"I love music," Luigi muttered. And he did. Music more than any other single thing in this world—except for Laura Lorenzini.

Who would not stop staring at her plate.

"We're in a pasta, all right," Luigi's father admitted.

(Note: that is not a misprint. Although in the rest of the world, the phrase is "we're in a pickle," they do not say that in Venice. All members of the cucumber family are looked on as bringing bad luck, but since spaghetti is very popular there, when they say they're in a quandary, Venetians admit to being "in a pasta," as Luigi's father did here.)

"I'm no quitter," Luigi said. "And here's what I'll do. I'll tie up at a spot on the Grand Canal tomorrow that no one else wants to use and I'll make a sign that says, 'Gondola for hire, rowing only.' That should do it."

Luigi's father shook his head. "It won't."

"Why not?"

"At the Gondolier's Tavern we were talking about you—as a matter of fact, that was all we talked about. You, Luigi. Fifty-seven women who live along the Grand Canal went to see their doctors this afternoon complaining of terrible headaches. You're very famous all of a sudden. I hate to tell you this, but you're a marked man."

"People forget," Luigi said, smiling his goony smile and looking with love at Laura Lorenzini.

The next morning he found his spot and made his sign.

And waited.

And waited.

He was hired twice in the afternoon—

—disaster—

—because even though he rowed magnificently and even though he didn't utter a single sound, he was pelted with trout, sea bass and all kinds of hard vegetables. It didn't matter, it seemed, that he didn't sing; all the people who lived facing the Grand Canal were afraid he might, and they wanted to head him off at the pass.

The next day he heard two women talking as they walked past his boat looking for a ride and one of them said, "Don't go near him, that's the garbage one."

He stuck to his post the rest of the week but he didn't earn enough for a can of Gondola Polish. At the end of the week, for the very first time, Luigi felt despair.

But at dinner his father was excited—"Great news," he announced.

Luigi said nothing, just toyed with his tortellini.

"At the Tavern today, a great plan was thought of. You're a very popular fellow, people like you." (This was true. It was impossible not to like Luigi.) "And we have found your salvation as a gondolier."

Luigi waited.

"Groups," his father explained, with mounting excitement. "When a party needs eight or twelve gondolas for a night row, we'll let you handle one of the boats. All the others will sing extra loud and you just smile and mouth the words and no one will know. Oh, Luigi, it's going to be perfect."

The first group row was ideal. Eight gondoliers, seven belting away, Luigi smiling and mouthing along. A triumph with extra tips for all.

If only it had lasted.

The second group was mammoth, *sixteen* gondolas, practically half the Grand Canal, and the other fifteen began singing *O Sole Mio* with remarkable power and precision—

—and then a young girl proclaimed in very loud tones to the group leader, "He isn't singing."

The group leader looked at the head gondolier "I paid for sixteen gondoliers, and it looks like you've brought in a ringer."

"He's been terribly sick. Throat surgery. He shouldn't be here now."

"Sing!" the group leader commanded.

Luigi did his best—

—chaos—

Fish from every window, shrieks from the passengers, tears from the children; the group leader ordered the gondolas to turn back, no one was paid.

That very night, an emergency session was held in the Gondolier's Tavern. George of the Gritti—the greatest of all gondoliers—summoned Luigi.

"Luigi," George of the Gritti said, "there is no time for beating around the tree." (Note: bushes are also considered bad luck in Venice.) "You are done. You're a nice fellow, we all admire your skill as an oarsman, but you are not only making us a laughing stock, you are costing us money. Your days as a gondolier are over, now and forever."

Luigi felt as if he had been killed. Or worse, as if Laura Lorenzini had broken off their engagement and scorned him as the worst failure ever to walk the earth. (This scene with Laura took place, in point of fact, as soon as the meeting was over and she heard the news.) "I'll die if I can't be a gondolier," Luigi said. And everyone in the room knew he was speaking the truth. "If I can't wake up in the morning and put on my gondolier's pants and my striped gondolier's shirt and row my gondola to work each day, if I can't do those things . . ." And now his voice trailed off.

"There are many wonderful jobs allied with the industry," George of the Gritti said. "You could be a guide and show tourists all the beautiful sights of the city. You could walk them through the museums. People like you, you'd be a great success."

"That's a wonderful idea," Luigi managed to say, "Thank you very much." He turned quickly and started to go.

"I have it," George of the Gritti cried then.
"You could *build* gondolas. No one understands
the boats as well as you and you're good with your
hands. I promise you here and now that if you
build me a gondola I will buy it and row it
with pride."

"Even a more valuable notion." Luigi nodded,
and he tried a smile and went to the door of the
Tavern.

But every man in the room knew he was
looking at a dead man.

"Hold," George of the Gritti said.

Luigi waited while there was a hurried
conference. Finally George of the Gritti said this:
"We have a solution, Luigi. You can wake up each
morning and put on your gondolier's pants and
your gondolier's shirt, all striped and pressed, and
you can row your gondola to work with your
head held high."

Luigi didn't know quite what to say. "Thank
you," he managed. "But what would my job be?"

George of the Gritti pointed to the tiny
windowless kitchen of the Tavern. "You could
work here. At the Gondolier's Tavern. You could
be the dishwasher for the rest of your natural life."

"How can I thank you," Luigi began. And he
ran and shook the hand of George of the Gritti. "I
accept, I accept, how lucky I am." Then he
hurried outside to tell his news to the waiting
night-black Laura Lorenzini . . .

V

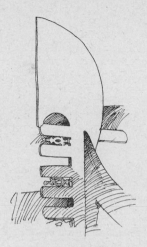

To find the Gondolier's
Tavern is at the same time
very easy and very hard.

The reason it's easy is because it's not that far
from the Grand Canal itself. You just take a
narrow unnamed canal where it touches the Grand,
turn right (or left, depending on which direction
you're coming from), row perhaps a quarter mile
and there it is.

The reason it's hard is because when you get to
the Gondolier's Tavern you go right past it. Not
only doesn't it have a sign of any kind out front,
it is also the kind of place you *know* you couldn't
be looking for. It is not very large (though not *that*
small) and kind of shaped like a squarish-rectangle
and it is the kind of blah color that no word has
yet been invented for. Except for the number of
gondolas parked in the canal all around it, there
is no way of knowing you have found your
destination.

We're Closed

And it isn't your
destination because no one—
let me underline that *no one*—
goes to the Gondolier's Tavern
except gondoliers
And it has been that way for
decades and decades.

The Tavern is run by a family with the
nickname of Porky. Porky XII was in charge then.
The family has terrible genes, and though they
start as gondoliers, by the time they reach perhaps
the age of thirty they are so fat they cannot row
anymore. So they work the bar. Which is why
the nickname.

There is only one item served in the Tavern and
that is a glorious light Venetian beer. (Gondoliers
are always thirsty from their labors, and they are,
along with the people of Australia, the greatest
consumers of beer per capita on the planet.)

When I was researching this, I was, because of
my family connections, allowed for one time only
into the Tavern to interview some men after work.
If you want to know why only gondoliers go there,

"we're thirsty."

let me tell you what
happened while I was
doing my interviewing.

The place was packed,
dozens of gondoliers
drinking pitchers of beer, and very noisy—
—suddenly, dead silence.

I spun around, surprised, and saw a wealthy-
looking English couple entering the place. Every
man in the place glared at the intruders. The
English couple looked around at the packed room
and then edged their way toward the bar itself.
"We're thirsty," the Englishman said.

"We're closed," Porky XII said.

The man turned to his wife. "Lively wit, these
Venetian peasants have," he said.

His wife, a very haughty-looking lady, nodded.

"What will you have, my dear," her lordly-
looking husband asked.

"Tea with lemon," she said.

"Jolly good idea," her husband replied, and he turned to Porky XII. "Two teas with lemon, freshly brewed, of course," he said.

"We are closed," Porky XII repeated, "and we have not served tea since the year 1822 and then it was by mistake."

The couple looked at each other, then around the silent room.

All the gondoliers still glared.

"I do adore these funny little bits of local color," the haughty English lady said.

"Goodbye and farewell," Porky XII said.

And now the lordly Englishman's face began to flush just a bit with pique. "Now look here," he said. "I am not without influence and I know my rights—clearly you are open and clearly we are thirsty—we will have what they are all having, and I want no more nonsense."

Porky XII nodded and reached under the bar and took out two gigantic pitchers and filled them both to the top. "These men are gondoliers," he said, "and they drink only horsepiss. That is all I serve—genuine Venetian horsepiss. I give you each a pitcher and I charge you nothing. But I promise you this—" and now he began advancing around the bar toward them. He weighed well over three hundred and fifty pounds, and even his mother acknowledged that his face had never been remotely cute. "I promise you that if you take one sip from your pitchers, *I will keep you here until you have drained every drop.*"

Watching what happened next, I must confess I was not surprised at the speed with which the lordly gentleman made his exit. But his wife, in high-heeled shoes, showed remarkable agility, screaming all the while as she left.

That was, I was told, as gentle as Porky XII is apt to get with intruders. Which is why there aren't a whole lot. Which is why gondoliers have flocked to the place forever. Surrounded by their friends, their fathers and cousins and sons, they drink vats of beer and swap lies with their intimates, while the rest of Venice glides by unknowing of the joys taking place inside.

Is it any wonder that the Gondolier's Tavern ranks as their third favorite building in all the world?

Second place, is, of course, their homes.

And in first?

Right next to the Gondolier's Tavern, touching it in fact, is the most ramshackle, nondescript tub of a structure you could imagine. But what you could not imagine is what it is.

A church.

A very special one, the most special one, at least to any gondolier. It is the Church of Souls of Those Who Died For the Sea.

And why is the Church of Souls of Those Who Died For the Sea so crucial? Well, you must understand this: gondoliers are like elephants—no one ever sees them die.

That's an exaggeration, of course. If a gondolier is taking a vacation, say, in Verona, and gets hit by a truck, obviously, he dies. Or if he's walking across the Piazza San Marco and succumbs to a fatal stroke—that's a public goodbye.

But accidents are the only exceptions. When a gondolier grows very old, too old to breathe much longer, or very sick, sick beyond the care of medical science, he mutters the words "I must visit my church."

And then his family carries him to his gondola. And they place him in it. And they hand him his oar. Or if he is too weak to grasp it, they strap the oar to his hand. And then they wave. And then, slowly, often painfully slowly, he moves his beloved oar and his boat gentles him away from his mooring place out toward the beckoning Adriatic Sea. This happens at night. Always. Always.

And when daylight comes, both boat and rider are gone. Never to be seen again. Not on this earth anyway. Where do gondoliers go? Nobody knows, any more than any man has ever seen the elephants' graveyard. This, of course, pertains only to their physical aspect. Everyone knows where the soul comes to permanent rest.

So you see now the reason for the ordering. The Gondolier's Tavern is third, because that is a place for pleasure.

And home is the place for love.

And the Church of Souls of Those Who Died For the Sea? Why, that is for ever . . .

VI

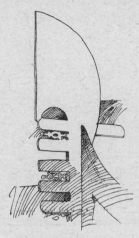

When Luigi went to work as the dishwasher of the Gondolier's Tavern, if you looked at him very very carefully, you would have known you were seeing a truly contented man. His attitude toward the world was as sunny as always; his goony smile never more evident.

Oh, in his early dishwashing days—

(*Note: his job title was* dishwasher *and that is how I refer to him in this research article, but there were no dishes in the place, only glasses that had once held beer, plus a large number of large pitchers. But Venetians, as I've said, are long on tradition, and at the turn of the century the Porky, who ran things then, read a cookbook one day and decided to serve food. He bought dishes and cooked away but everything he made made you gag so, the place reverted to its purely liquid menu. The job title, as I've indicated, remained.)*

In Luigi's early days, there were a few rough moments, all supplied by John the Bastard, his former teacher at the School, who always shouted, "Sing for us," when he entered the place or "How's our singing dishwasher today?" or "I've been invited to Laura Lorenzini's engagement party, Luigi, of course, I'll see you there." (Laura married the great young gondolier Donald of the Danieli within six months of Luigi's starting to work.)

These remarks irritated the crowd—everybody liked Luigi—and, to a man, they admitted that for seamanship no one could touch him in a gondola. At first, there were stares at John the Bastard, who went on with his stinging, and then a few men asked him please to stop, but John the Bastard was tough.

His taunts came to an abrupt end one day when Porky VIII took him aside and said, "*Sei non stai zitto mi siederò sulla tua testa e ne farò una pizza!*" which in rough equivalent means, "If you don't shut up I'm going to sit on your head and make a pizza of it!"

No more stings from that day forth.

And everyone was jovial with Luigi and he smiled and laughed and talked with everybody when there were enough clean glasses.

A potentially difficult situation, in other words, had been cleanly handled, all pain averted.

In truth, of course, Luigi's heart was shredded. No one knew. You could not know. There was no way, such was his skill at putting a good sweet face on things.

I mentioned earlier that Luigi had secrets, lots of little ones and one great one. His Great Secret was his only dream and it was this: just for once in his life to be allowed to sing his lungs out on the Grand Canal.

No, it was more than that.

Not just his lungs. He wanted to be able to sing his lungs and his heart out on the Grand Canal.

No, it was more than that.

Not just his lungs and his heart. He wanted to be able to have the glorious privilege and opportunity to sing with his entire being. He wanted to sing his lungs out and his heart out and his soul out on the Grand Canal.

For hours. Perhaps even one entire magical night. Just be there, on the most glorious street ever imagined by the mind of man. In his very own gondola. Singing all the most beautiful songs ever written by Verdi and Puccini and Rossini.

It was inconceivable, of course. He would be buried under tons of fish and cabbage and carrots and broccoli and every hard vegetable one could think of. People would have headaches that would last forever.

There are many bad things about the human race. But there are many good things too. And one of the best is this—dreams, great dreams, die hard . . .

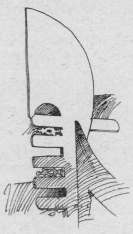

I must now talk briefly about the next ten years of Luigi's life.

He worked daily at the Tavern, washing glasses and pitchers and sometimes answering the old telephone they kept in one corner. The phone was used only by the wives of gondoliers, calling up to find their husbands. There was a very strict code that no wife was allowed to call in until her man had been gone at least twenty-four hours. By that time, the wives were either very angry or very hysterical or, most often, both.

They would call and scream: "What miserable cur is this speaking?" And Luigi would politely respond, "Luigi," and then the wife would say, "Well you're probably a bum too, Luigi, you stink, Luigi, let me talk to Tony right away or I will kill you both." And Luigi would do as he was told.

He averaged three wife abuses per day, but he kept his goony smile on because that was part of the job.

The Tavern opened at nine in the morning for any gondoliers who felt the need of a little throat soother before tackling the tourists, and Luigi opened the bar. It closed at three in the morning and Luigi always closed the bar. Eighteen hours a day, always with his smile on.

He had taken a tiny room near the Tavern—his mother's shame had mandated that he not ever come home anymore—and that was where he slept.

But he didn't sleep much.

Because each night, after he closed the Tavern, when all of Venice was dark and snoring, he would creep to the canal and his gondola. Then in the chill black darkness he would silently guide his gondola out into the Adriatic Sea.

And there he would sing.

He would sing and he would practice with his gondola. He got very skilled with his gondola. (He already was very skilled with it, and I don't want to overstate this, but the fact is, in those cold cold black hours, he came close to being a magician. Those whom I interviewed who were to be trusted all agreed on one point: Luigi could make his gondola dance.)

The singing, of course, was what kept him at it. It wasn't his great dream, naturally. Singing on the Grand Canal, singing your heart and lungs and soul out on the most legendary street in the world, is a far cry from singing in the Adriatic in the middle of the night.

But it kept his dream, however fitfully, alive.

Then, at dawn, when the first fishermen were silhouetted in the distance, Luigi got quickly quiet and just as quickly went home to his room. As the city awakened, he fell asleep.

That was how the ten years passed.

Until, one startling day, Luigi disappeared.

VIII

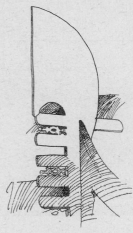

The following years of Luigi's life were the most difficult for me to research. So many years had gone by, so few clues to work with. But being a writer, as I've been all my adult life, teaches you the virtues of patience. And at last, I received a hand-written note from a niece of The Great Sorrento and I traveled to Rome to interview her.

She showed me Sorrento's journals for the years in question, and at last I can fairly well reconstruct what happened.

The Great Sorrento was not short on ego. He was born Richard (Riccardo) Sorrento, but when his pupils began getting famous, he became furious because the critics only wrote about his pupils and not about him. So he went to court and had his name legally changed from "Richard" to "The Great." This brought him a great deal of notoriety and by the time Luigi went to see him, The Great Sorrento was the best-known voice teacher in Italy, France, Spain, not to mention the rest of the world.

He was even more greedy than he was famous.

"I want to sing," Luigi told him.

"So does every dog and cat on the Piazza Navona," replied The Great Sorrento.

"It is my life's ambition," Luigi said.

"Speak up," The Great said. "I can't hear you when you whisper like that."

"I'm very nervous," Luigi explained.

"I do that to people," The Great Sorrento said. "I don't know if it's my legendary skills or the sheer force of my dazzling personality. Probably a combination of both. Speak now and louder."

"My life is over if I cannot sing."

"That at least shows you have a certain interest in learning," The Great Sorrento said. His enormous studio overlooked Trevi Fountain and he wandered to the windows and looked at the view.

"I have saved every penny for ten years praying for such a moment," Luigi said. "Please say you will take me on as a pupil."

"Ten years, eh? How much have you saved?"

Luigi emptied his little bag of all its cash. "Two thousand."

Sorrento liked the sound of that. He went to his desk and got out a legal-looking document and a quill pen. "I am a very severe taskmaster," he said. "You will sign this paper. It says you give me the two thousand now and I will teach you. If I am too hard on you—and I will be—and you decide to quit after a few lessons, I will have your money, so my time will not have been wasted."

Luigi signed.

"We have a deal, you may call me Your Great, let's get down to business."

"Yes, Your Great," Luigi said. "And bless you."

"Do you know any Italian operas?"

"All of them, every one I think, by heart."

Sorrento looked closely at the man in the gondolier's clothes. "You interest me," he said finally. "*The Barber of Seville*. Sing."

Luigi could not control the trembling of his hands, so he clasped them tightly together, closed his eyes, and started to sing:

"*Ecco ridente in cielo, spunta la bella aurora . . .*"

He sang for at least fifteen seconds before The Great Sorrento charged at him and put his hands over Luigi's mouth. Then he sank into a chair.

"You don't interest me," he said finally, when he could breathe easily again.

"I was very nervous, Your Great. I'll get better."

"The reverse is not possible," Sorrento said. He pointed to the door— "Take your money and go."

Luigi did a very brave thing. He held up the contract and pointed to his signature. "We are legally bound together."

The Great Sorrento ripped the contract in half.

"I'm not leaving," Luigi said.

"I'm not teaching," Sorrento said.

"It's my life if you don't, Your Great."

"It's *my* life if I do," Sorrento replied.

They went on like that for a while, Luigi begging one way, Sorrento begging the other, until finally they came to an agreement. Sorrento gave Luigi his money back and two thousand in addition if Luigi promised never to come back again. He also gave Luigi a letter to Cristaldi, the second best teacher in Rome.

Cristaldi gave Luigi another two thousand to go away.

By the time he had worked his way through all the best teachers in Rome, Luigi had made a lot of money—fifteen thousand in all—but his poor flickering dream was starting to fade.

The Pickle proved his salvation.

The Pickle—Piccoli was his last name—lived in a basement in an abandoned area near the Naples waterfront. He was a hundred and six years old, and everyone thought he was dead. As a matter of fact, he looked dead and didn't move much. But once, half a century before, singers had flocked to him from all across the world.

Luigi heard about him by rumor and tracked him to his lonely basement. The Pickle handed Luigi some paper and a pen. "You are my last chance," Luigi wrote. "If you cannot teach me, I don't know what will happen."

"Sing," The Pickle said.

Luigi sang.

"There is much work to be done," The Pickle said when Luigi was finished.

Luigi blinked. "You mean you'll take me?" he wrote.

The Pickle nodded.

"And teach me to be a great singer?" he scribbled.

"I cannot promise 'great,' " The Pickle said.
" 'Better' I can promise. 'Much improved' is in
the bag. But you'll have to work."

Luigi began to write that he would work hard,
harder than anyone ever had worked before, so
hard in fact— He stopped writing and, instead,
took the old man's hand and brought it to his
lips and kept it there a while.

The Pickle had a spare room behind his
basement quarters and it was arranged immediately
for Luigi to move in. That night, the old man
explained that the basis of Luigi's problem was
simple: he was singing wrong.

To sing correctly, you must sing from the
diaphragm. To sing correctly, your voice must
have focus. To sing correctly, you must understand
that singing is simply speaking supported on
pitch. To sing correctly, you must sing with ease.

Luigi wrote "I see" and "Oh how brilliant"
and "I never knew that" and all kinds of other such
replies. (The reason he wrote his answers, by the
way, was that The Pickle had lost all hearing
twenty-five years before, which had damaged his
practice. Luigi was the first pupil he had had for
a decade.)

But his mind was still sharp. He liked Luigi
and he gave him a series of demanding exercises.
Luigi was to sing scales half an hour every day.
(Luigi sang scales half an hour every hour.)

He had to strengthen his diaphragm by
holding five-pound weights in his hands while
he sang. (Luigi was holding fifty-pound weights
in his hands within a month.) Luigi had to learn

to hang upside down from the doorway so his tone would improve. But not more than a few minutes because of the blood rushing to the head. (Luigi learned not to mind the blood and after a few weeks he could not pass a doorway without hanging upside down.) Luigi had to have pasta for lunch and dinner every day because nothing gave focus to the voice as quickly as pasta. (Luigi had pasta for breakfast, as well as for the other meals, and he could tell immediately how his focus was improving.)

In fact, he could tell that everything was improving: his strength, his placing of the voice, his diaphragm use. The old man said he had never had as willing a student.

But Luigi had to master emotions as well. His hands, his body, the look in his eyes. So every afternoon they had emotion class, and The Pickle, stern as he was, was delighted.

They studied together for five years. Day and night and day. The Pickle was one hundred and eleven when he kissed Luigi on both cheeks and told him he was ready.

Luigi wasn't sure.

"Go," the old man told him. "Go thrill the world."

Luigi still wasn't sure. But with his fingers very much crossed, he returned to Venice. He had no real hopes of thrilling the world; all he truly prayed for was that it would stop laughing at him . . .

IX

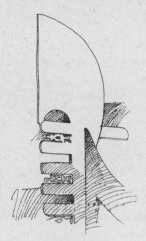

"Can I have a gondola ride, please, mister?"

Luigi's father, old and dozing in his spot in front of the Ignazione Hotel, suddenly came alive. He jumped to his feet, ran and embraced his son. Then he took a step away and looked at his child's face. Definitely Luigi, the same goony smile. "We thought you were gone forever."

"Just not a very good letter writer," Luigi replied.

"You're still wearing your gondolier's costume."

"Always; what else in the world is better?"

"Where have you been—what have you been doing—?"

"I've been traveling all over Europe," Luigi said casually. "I've been on a five-year vacation, just having fun."

"You haven't been doing anything?"

Luigi shook his head. "Enjoying myself. Taking it easy. I worked very hard at the Tavern and I saved my money. It was wonderful, relaxing, without a care in the world." He looked over his father's shoulder. "Your gondola looks better than ever."

"I've been taking care of yours too; it's tied up back at the house. I waxed it whenever I did mine."

"Thank you," Luigi said. It was a sunny November afternoon; the Grand Canal sparkled.

"I suppose you're going home now to surprise the family," Luigi's father said.

Luigi stretched and yawned. "Soon, father; but it's so pretty here I thought I might just chat with you for a while."

Luigi never had all that much to talk to his father about, but he stayed with the old man for two hours—business was very slow, the month being what it was, and after a while, the pauses in their conversation became longer and longer.

But finally, at three o'clock, an old couple tottered out of the Ignazione and asked for a gondola ride.

Luigi's father hopped to it, helping them in, getting them comfortable, untying his rope, grabbing his oar.

That was when Luigi spoke, his voice as steady as could be: "Daddy," he said. "What about if *I* took them? Just for old times' sake."

Luigi's father hesitated.

"I'm sure I remember how to use the oar."

"No one ever used it better, I'm not worried about that."

"Good," Luigi said, and he took the oar and

skipped nimbly to the rear of the gondola. "Push me off?"

"Be careful," was all Luigi's father said.

And then Luigi was out on the Grand Canal. "Where may I take you?" he asked the old couple.

"We'd like to see the Piazza San Marco from the water."

"A perfect choice," Luigi said, and he expertly turned the gondola, pointing it up toward the Piazza. His hands caressed the oar as if they had been working every day. He moved the gondola so that it didn't so much as wiggle, even when other boats passed close by. Luigi seemed, when viewed from the outside, in a state of absolute calm.

But inside, out of all control, his heart was pounding because he sensed, no, he knew—knew without doubt—that all his life was simply a preamble to what was about to come.

The old couple began to whisper.

Now the old man will turn, Luigi thought.

The old man turned.

And now he'll clear his throat.

The old man made a throat-clearing sound.

"Yes, I'd be delighted," Luigi said.

The old man looked puzzled. "I haven't asked anything yet."

"Sorry," Luigi muttered. Fool, he told himself; relax. Calm. *Calm.*

"Would you sing for us?" the old man asked then.

"Yes, I'd be delighted."

"Do you know *O Sole Mio*?"

"I think I've heard it, yes, sir."

"Do it then, we would like that." He turned and put his arm around his wife.

Luigi tensed. But then he commanded himself to stop—tension was the enemy of song. Being tense did terrible things to your muscles: you could not project properly if tension lurked inside you.

He took a deep breath. Another. Slowly he could feel the tension draining from his body.

And then blessed calm took over.

It had been fifteen years since he had rowed with a passenger along the Grand Canal. But the last five of those had not been wasted. He thought of The Pickle, heard the one-hundred-plus-year-old voice: "Get your balance, Luigi. Make sure your feet are comfortable. Make sure your body is comfortable. You are floating. Do not fear your diaphragm. Make it obey your wishes. Get your focus, do not forget how easy it all is. Remember, singing is nothing in the world but speaking on a higher pitch. Take a breath. Close your eyes. Take another breath. Think of all the voices that have thrilled you in your lifetime. Think of your mother humming lullabies, think of all the choirs in all the churches of the world, think of the great gondoliers, think of nothing now but the sound, think of all the years of hanging upside down, of walking around with fifty-pound weights in your hands. Now the sound again, think of the sound, your sound, your own very special sound. Take another breath. Deeper. Deeper. All right. We are ready. Open your eyes. Smile—your emotions are right. Your body is right. Your diaphragm is your friend. You are ready. You alone can thrill the world. Do so, my child; do so now . . ."

It was eleven minutes past three. Luigi opened his eyes and took a perfect breath. And then, at last, he sang . . .

MYSTERY

A mysterious ailment swept the Piazza San Marco at shortly after three o'clock today.

Seventeen men and women who were strolling near the Grand Canal suddenly were overcome and collapsed. All complained of stomach cramps and head pains.

They were rushed to nearby hospitals where they remained overnight for observation. Hospital authorities were baffled as to the cause, although one expert suspected it might have been due to a poorly mixed batch of *Tartufo*.

A spokesman for one hospital said, "We must give thanks that this happened in November; if it had taken place during the height of the tourist season, we might have been faced with an international catastrophe." Investigation is continuing . . .

From the
VENICE POST GAZETTE
November 20th.

X

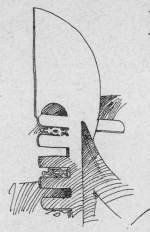

Clearly, those of us who have come this far in the narrative know the cause wasn't *Tartufo*.

Was The Pickle a fraud then?

Not at all. He had taken an untutored dishwasher and taught him the proper way to sing. Unfortunately, being deaf, he could not evaluate the quality of sound coming from his student, only that it was produced in a correct manner.

And Luigi did sing perfectly now—and with easily three times the power than before he took to studying.

The sound, alas, was also three times as bad.

Luigi returned immediately to the Gondolier's Tavern. His job was taken, but out of the goodness of his ample heart, Porky VIII gave him the post of Assistant Dishwasher, at half his old salary. Luigi smiled and thanked him and went to work at once. He seemed the same old good fellow. And he was. Except now he had no dreams.

This, as stated, happened on the 20th of November. Exactly one month later, on the 20th of December, the weather began what is still referred to as The Four Day Whirlwind . . .

XI

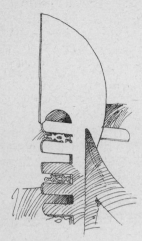

Perhaps the biggest gaffe I made during all of my interviews took place when I talked with the head of the Venice Meteorological Service and casually asked him, at the start, if he would mind talking about The Four Day Whirlwind.

He minded.

"It was not a whirlwind," he shouted. "We do not have whirlwinds in Venice. There never has been one and there never will be one."

"What was it then?" I asked.

He sighed. He was a little fat fellow and had been weatherman for Venice for many years. His office was filled with frightening-looking maps. "*This*," he said, "is a whirlwind." And he made a circular gesture with his index finger. "See? Round."

I understood that much and said so.

"Now *this* is what took place on those four days," he went on, and this time he made a square with his index finger. "We had a breeze from the north in Austria and we had a breeze from the south in Sicily, and we had a breeze from the east in Yugoslavia and we had a breeze from the west in France."

"All four breezes at once?" I asked.

"Very unusual." He nodded. "We weathermen call it by its official title: *The Four Day Four Country Rectangular Aerial Disturbance*. My father named it that; he was the weatherman then. On the second day when he was coming to work he was blown all the way up through a window on the third floor of the Doge's Palace."

"We agree then at least that it was bad weather."

"Oh it was a bitch all right," the Meteorological Service man said. "But—and please get this across to your readers—it was not a whirlwind."

Whatever it was, it was not good for Venice.

Few cities decorate for the holidays more beautifully, green and blue and red lights alternating all around the Piazza San Marco, all along the Grand Canal. Up until December 20th, the stringers were working as usual.

On the 20th, there was only the wind, so the stringers did their best to get everything in perfect readiness. The second day the wind got stronger, and the rain began, and the town council decided to delay any further holiday decoration, since everything you put up blew down. The third day the rain got stronger and Venice began to flood.

The fourth day most of the city was three feet under water.

People stayed inside, huddled and waiting for a change in the atmosphere. Hardly anybody dared to go outside.

Except the gondoliers—they *all* went outside until they reached the Tavern. Then they ducked in and began drinking pitchers of beer. The Tavern stayed open around the clock, and it had never been as full. The Chief Dishwasher collapsed from exhaustion, putting extra pressure on Luigi to keep up. He did his best, never going to sleep for even a minute while the whirlwind (or whatever you want to call it) held the city captive.

His only rest came twice each day when he hurried to the tubby building next door, the Church of Souls of Those Who Died For the Sea, where he prayed for the dead and for the dead yet to come. For surely there would be many. The small back canals were dangerous enough. The Grand Canal was impossible.

Except for the Giant Fireboat.

The Giant Fireboat was the mightiest ship in all of Europe. It stayed in the Venice Firehouse at the far end of the Grand Canal, more than a mile from the Church. Throughout the four days of the whirlwind, it was rarely at rest. The people in Venice, those in dire trouble, could only be rescued by the Great Fireboat—not necessarily from fire, but from the possibility of drowning when the waters rose too high.

Luigi prayed for the Giant Fireboat too, prayed that nothing ill would come to it during this terrible time.

Then he would rush back to the Tavern and get to work. And there had never been such work to do because never had so many gondoliers been in one place and drunk so much beer for so long a time.

"Luigi, more glasses, more pitchers," Porky VIII would shout, and Luigi would come scurrying out of the tiny kitchen area balancing as many trays as he could. "More, more, more, you lazy fool," Porky VIII would bellow, and Luigi did his best. He kept his goony smile on just as often as he could, and though his arms ached and his back hurt and his legs cramped, he kept at his job. Not a single rest for all the ninety-six hours.

As I said, the whirlwind began on the 20th of December and did not end until the 24th. But when it ended, there was not much joy in Venice—

—because on the 24th, the Adriatic Sea went mad, and the Killer Storm began . . .

XII

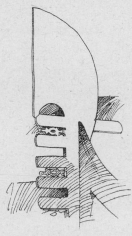

Venice is thousands of years old and in all its history, there had been nothing to equal the Killer Storm. By noon of that December 24th, the water level stood at six feet. An hour later, it rose a foot more. And that was just the start. All the windows in Venice have wooden shields in case of bad weather—these wooden shields were as effective as toothpicks. Waves on the Grand Canal were ten feet high and devastated buildings.

Then in mid-afternoon, the thunder and lightning began. (Not precisely true—of course there had been thunder and lightning in the morning, but it was the kind of weather condition we've all experienced before. You know, a rumble, then a few minutes later, another rumble perhaps accompanied by a bolt from the heavens. That kind of thing.) But in mid-afternoon, they became continuous. The sound made children scream, and there was no pause between the rumbles. And the lightning kept it company, making the besieged city bright as day.

In the Tavern, the gondoliers drank and talked about other weather they had seen. They boasted of much worse conditions they had lived through. They topped one another with terrible descriptions of typhoons and hurricanes and more. But their boasts were hollow. They were lying to one another and though none of them would admit it, they all knew it to be true. No one had ever been near weather like this and who knew what would be left of their golden city when it ended?

The hours went on as the storm increased: they drank more because the thunder made it very difficult to hear anyone who didn't shout into your ear. The lightning seemed to be growing close, but that was impossible since it was all around them anyhow. They were sitting on tables now—on chairs on top of tables, more accurately, because the water level was rising in the Tavern. Luigi sloshed from the kitchen to the bar with his trays. The beer faucets were open like water hoses.

It was very hard to think that anything could get much worse, and in point of fact, nothing did get much worse.

Until close to midnight. When a lightning bolt started a fire in the roof of the Church of Souls of Those Who Died For the Sea.

Porky VIII was the first to spot the smoke. He screamed and pointed and everybody jumped down from their chairs on top of the tables and went to the windows and stared. For a moment no one spoke. Then George of the Gritti, the wisest

and bravest as well as the greatest gondolier, told everybody to relax. It was a small fire now, and all they had to do was phone the Firehouse at the end of the Grand Canal and the Great Fireboat would come and that would be the end of their troubles.

And so it would have been. No question.

Except the phone was dead, killed by the Killer Storm.

There followed a moment of genuine panic in the Tavern. The fire was starting to spread in the Church, and nothing but the Great Fireboat could stop it. But the boat was a mile away and there are few streets in Venice and they were covered with ten feet of water now.

Then everyone turned and stared at George of the Gritti. Someone would have to travel the Grand Canal and quickly—and that someone could only be George.

He smiled, finished his pitcher of beer, and made a gesture of fierce triumph. "Don't you dare run out of beer while I'm gone."

With that he was out the door and running toward his tied-up gondola. The wind knocked him down but he got right up. It knocked him down again but again he got up. He reached his gondola, put his hands on the rope—

—and came quietly back inside.

He was pale and shaking and he looked at no one. He managed to say, "More beer," and he took a pitcher and drank it all. He stared down and all the others stared away. As he gazed into the empty pitcher, George seemed suddenly small and suddenly old. That is what fear can do to even the bravest of men.

Donald of the Danieli was the one they turned to next. He ranked only behind George and, many felt, would soon supplant him. Donald nodded, went to the door, moved out into the Killer Storm.

He looked briefly up to the roof of the Church.

Now there were flames.

He broke into a run toward his gondola while inside everyone cheered and shouted his name, and no one can be sure what went through Donald's mind, perhaps his beautiful wife, Laura Lorenzini, perhaps their five young children.

But he only got a third of the way toward his craft when he spun around and fled back into the Tavern.

Dead silence. He climbed back onto his chair on top of the table and emptied his pitcher of beer.

There was no blame, understand. All the gondoliers understood that there are limits to what the human mind can endure. The men stood by the windows and watched as the Church flames grew, and the thunder rumbled and the lightning grew only brighter. The gondoliers drank and drank and finally Porky VIII shouted, "More glasses, more glasses and pitchers, Luigi, *more glasses and pitchers right now!*"

No answer.

Porky cursed and dashed into the kitchen.

No Luigi.

Silence again.

Then someone saw.

Lit by lightning, a single figure was ripping at the ropes on his gondola, grabbing his oar and pushing off. And then one lone black boat began moving, slowly, yes, but moving, moving into the Killer Storm toward the Grand Canal . . .

XIII

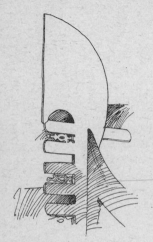

Luigi knew what he had to do—

—correction, sorry—

—Luigi knew what he had *to try* to do, which was to travel on the small canal the hundreds of yards till it met with the Grand—and then to turn and row a mile to the Firehouse. He took one final glance back to his beloved tub of a church—

—the flames were higher now.

No question that Luigi absolutely understood the task before him. What he didn't know was, was it possible? And even if it was, even if he could somehow reach the Firehouse and alert the Great Fireboat, would it reach the tubby building in time to save it?

The thunder roared, and Luigi squinted so that the cutting rain would not attack his eyes quite as sharply. The lightning was so bright he could have

read the paper if he'd had one. But of course, he
didn't have one. What he had was his gondola
and his single oar—

—and it didn't seem enough.

He was going so slowly, much much too slowly.
He almost turned again to see his Church but he
didn't, because he didn't want to know how high
the flames were now.

And no matter how hard he tried, he did not
seem able to go faster. Up ahead, perhaps no more
than a few hundred yards, was the Grand Canal
itself.

But getting there seemed beyond him.

Have I forgotten my gondola skills? He
wondered. Were all those ten years of night
practice alone for nothing? True, he had been away
from his boat, but you never forgot how to make
your gondola obey you. And true, he'd been
studying singing for five years. But in those years
he'd hung thousands of hours upside down on
doors, so his legs were stronger than ever, and he'd
stood for thousands of more hours with fifty-pound
weights in his hands, so his arms were stronger
than ever.

He gripped his oar so tightly now that his
hands began to bleed. He bent his body forward and
dug in with his oar with all the power of his
mighty arms. He increased the length of his
rowing motion; he increased the speed of his oar
as it cut into the water. He was already into his
second wind and kept working and kept working—

—too too slow.

The Grand Canal was still well over a hundred
yards away.

Luigi closed his eyes and fought the water. Stroke! he told himself. Stroke! Again! Again! Deeper! Again! Stroke!

He opened his eyes and all that effort was beginning to be worthwhile—he *was* going faster.

At last, at last.

Luigi had but a moment to reflect on his good fortune. Because suddenly he realized it was not good fortune at all, but the reverse.

He was going too fast now.

He was out of control.

The Grand Canal was sucking him forward, the currents pulling him at a speed he had never dreamed of going—

—and then he was caught in the maelstrom of the Grand Canal itself.

Luigi stared around and cried out.

But no one heard his cry because the thunder was echoing off the shattering palaces, making it impossible for anyone to hear anything.

And the lightning stung his eyes; it was a living terror ruling the surface of the water.

Again Luigi cried out and again no one heard.

A giant wave had him now—a giant wave with a white crest—and it lifted him twenty feet up into the air and then another giant wave took control and he was thirty feet up in the air and then the biggest wave he had ever seen caught him and spun his tiny boat. He was helpless atop the fifty-foot wave and for a moment it toyed with him.

The Killer Storm was too great an enemy. He could not do battle against an enemy of such power.

The fifty-foot wave took its time, spinning him as he stood desperately trying to keep his balance on the back of his gondola.

Then the wave, perhaps bored, who knows, no one will ever know, ended the spinning and started toward a nearby palace, and Luigi watched as a smaller wave smashed against the palace and then a thirty-footer smashed against the palace and now the fifty-foot wave was roaring down toward the palace wall carrying Luigi with it and all he could think of was that he had failed—nothing new, he had always failed.

But then another thought replaced it, and Luigi grabbed for the thought as the wave came nearer to the hard stone walls of the palace; he held to the thought as he, helpless, rode closer and closer to his end, and that thought was that at least he would die a gondolier's death, at least he would die for the sea . . .

XIV

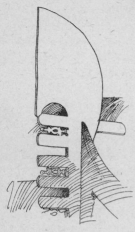

I must now digress for a moment, in the interests of scholarly and historical accuracy, and discuss, albeit briefly, the lives of three famous Americans, namely Mark Spitz, Johnny Weismuller, and Duke P. Kahanamoku.

Mark Spitz, of course, was the young Indiana University graduate, who stunned the sports world in the 1972 Olympics. What Spitz did was win seven gold medals in seven different swimming races and, in the course of that action, set seven new world records. Truly amazing. (He later went on to a less successful career in the field of entertainment.) And when writers in 1972 were discussing Spitz' achievements, when they ran out of adjectives, whom did they compare Spitz to?

Why, Johnny Weismuller, of course.

Weismuller is primarily remembered today for the series of movies in which he played Tarzan the Ape Man. But before that, he was also truly amazing in the water. Example? He was never beaten in any free-style race from 100 yards to one-half mile. No one else in history ever came close to approximating that. And when writers in the 1920s were discussing Weismuller's achievements, when they ran out of adjectives, whom did they compare Weismuller to?

None other than the Hawaiian wonder, Duke P. Kahanamoku.

Like the others, Kahanamoku also set myriad world records and won many Olympic titles. The Duke (as he was always referred to) also went into the entertainment field.
Without overwhelming success.

But—

—do you know of that sport, I think it's officially called surfboarding, that is so popular now in tropical areas? I'm sure you've seen it on television. Today it's done with short boards that are perhaps six or eight feet long made of lightweight plastic.

Well, the Duke was the father of surfboarding. His board is on display today in the Bishop Museum in Honolulu. It would take two strong men to lift it, although the Duke, a giant of a man, did it himself. It is fifteen feet long and made entirely of wood.

The reason the Duke is the father is not primarily because he was the first man who ever attempted surfboarding. Rather, it is because he was the first man who ever thought of moving up and down the length of the board, for better balance and longer rides.

If you read his memoirs, you'll know where he got the idea . . .

XV

Who among us is wise
enough to understand the
mind of man? I have spent
a lifetime in such pursuit and find myself no closer
to solution now than when I was a boy. Why do
great ideas come? What causes those sudden
illuminations of the spirit? Newton needed the
apple to jar his mind.

Luigi's great idea was not as scientifically
important, but it meant a lot to Luigi. And why
it came when it did, with the fifty-foot wave
hurling him to destruction against the palace wall,
I have not the least way of presuming. But his idea
was startling, and it was this: the Killer Storm
was not his enemy. Rather the reverse; it was the
greatest gift ever given him.

But if he was to receive his gift he first had to
survive. So as his gondola tipped and as the palace
wall came close enough for him to count the stones,

he scurried from his position at the rear of the gondola and tiptoed along the railing toward the center of his craft in order to try to save his balance.

And the gondola swerved into a sharp turn, and he spun away from death.

Hmmm, Luigi thought, I wonder why that happened? Odd. Was it a one-time thing or could I do it again?

The opportunity for further investigation came immediately, as another giant wave gripped his boat, and rushed it across the canal, toward the palaces on the other side.

Halfway there, Luigi skipped to the front of his gondola—

—and again the gondola curved away from destruction.

Interesting, Luigi thought.

But he didn't get a chance to think much more because now a bigger wave than any yet took hold of his boat—perhaps it was sixty feet of foaming power, and so loud that it almost matched the constant thunder—and when Luigi was at the crest it spun him, and when it had him spinning it rolled him toward the Gritti Palace Hotel itself, toward what was left of its grandeur. Surely Luigi would have perished there if he had not used his oar for balance and raced to the rear of his boat where the wave lost its hold on him.

I can ride these monsters, Luigi realized, as another monster took hold of his small black boat, and it spun him and—

—correction, sorry—

—as it *tried* to spin him. But Luigi jumped to the middle rail and balanced, leaning far out into the wind, and another wave had failed in its attack.

And now all the hours of being alone in the dark on his gondola took over; those ten terrible years of solitude gave him confidence, because suddenly he was not just riding the monsters, he was doing something even more incredible—he was taming them, making them do what he wanted. And what he wanted then was to race down the Grand Canal to the Firehouse and that is just what he did. Wave after wave attacked him, but he conquered them all, moving back and forth like a dancer now, his balance perfect, his hands moving his oar with the same ease of a conductor moving his baton; and he soared down the canal,

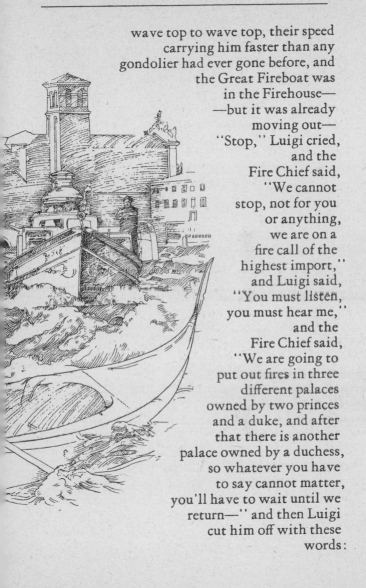

wave top to wave top, their speed
carrying him faster than any
gondolier had ever gone before, and
the Great Fireboat was
in the Firehouse—
—but it was already
moving out—
"Stop," Luigi cried,
and the
Fire Chief said,
"We cannot
stop, not for you
or anything,
we are on a
fire call of the
highest import,"
and Luigi said,
"You must listen,
you must hear me,"
and the
Fire Chief said,
"We are going to
put out fires in three
different palaces
owned by two princes
and a duke, and after
that there is another
palace owned by a duchess,
so whatever you have
to say cannot matter,
you'll have to wait until we
return—" and then Luigi
cut him off with these
words:

"The Church of Souls of Those Who Died
For the Sea is in flames," and the Fire Chief stood
there a moment, blinking, before he whirled on
his men and hollered, "The Gondoliers' Church
is on fire, pray we're not too late," and he and

Luigi talked for a minute more only and then the Great Fireboat of Venice was roaring full throttle up the Grand Canal and when it reached the Church all the expert firemen raced into action and when the fire was out the gondoliers embraced the firemen and George of the Gritti blessed the Fire Chief because not too long before, he, George, had been faced with a life full in the knowledge that he was, at heart, nothing but a coward but now those thoughts need not bother him so much and he hugged the Fire Chief and lifted him off the ground and kissed him on both cheeks which didn't please the Fire Chief all that much, but he understood that people sometimes act strangely when emergencies crop up and then George said, looking around, "Luigi?" and the Fire Chief said, "Who is Luigi, my name is Leon," and George said, "Luigi is a gondolier," and Leon the Fire Chief said, "All you gondoliers look alike to me, did this one have kind of a goony smile?" and George nodded and the Fire Chief said, "At the very end, after he'd told us about the Church, I asked him to come on board but he said he had someplace very important to go."

George shook his head. "But where? Where could a man need to go while the Killer Storm rages?" and then that question spread through all the gondoliers. "Where, where on this night, could Luigi be?"

I can answer that question, and it seems to me only fair that I do so now . . .

99

XVI

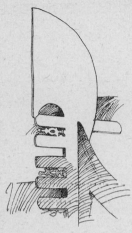

Luigi was in a place
few of us are fortunate
enough to ever visit: he
was living inside his dream.

You see, back when the first fifty-footer grabbed
him and spun him and tried to dash him against
the palace wall, that was when he realized what a
great friend he had in the Killer Storm.

Why?

Because such was its power, so great the
pounding of the constant thunder, that he
understood this: at last, for once and for the only
time, he could rove the Grand Canal and no one
could hear him sing.

And so he left the Great Fireboat to do its job while he rode the waves back to the center of the Grand Canal, and the rain cut at his face but he loved it, and the lightning tried to knife him but he loved that too; most of all, though, he loved the deafening thunder. He could sing his lungs out now. He could sing his lungs out and his heart out now. He could sing his lungs and heart and most of all his tattered soul out now, and who was to know? No one, not on this Christmas morning.

He began to ride the waves, alone on the Grand Canal, riding up and down its length, and he thought of The Pickle and he remembered his lessons, and his balance was perfect, and his diaphragm had never obeyed him so easily, and his focus would have made the old teacher smile and nod in appreciation.

Luigi sang. He sang solos from Bellini and he sang solos from Verdi and he sang all the solos that he knew—and, of course, he knew them all—and then he sang duets, first one part, then the other; and he knew all the duets too, and the trios and the quartets. It didn't matter how loud he sang, the blessed thunder sheltered him, and the night went on with Luigi flashing along the great waterway, curving his boat from wave to giant wave, and he closed his eyes when he wanted to and he opened them when he wanted to and out it came, all the song, all the music he had harbored forever inside. It poured from his throat, note following note, hour following hour. If he thought of anything besides his music it was that of all men, surely he was the most fortunate.

There were many things he paid no attention to that night. Perhaps most important was this: from corners, behind buildings, men were watching him—all of them gondoliers. At first they were stunned at the sight of the tiny craft riding the waves, and they were afraid that Luigi would drown, but then they realized there was no reason for fear: that lone man out there, the single small figure whose mouth seemed to be opening and closing all the while, the Christmas gondolier was safe within the storm.

By dawn the storm was ending. As soon as the thunder began to quiet, so did Luigi. He hurried back to the Tavern and began washing glasses and pitchers.

None of the other gondoliers talked much to him. But there can be no question that they all looked at him somewhat strangely . . .

XVII

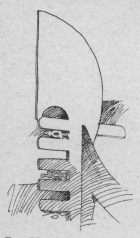

By the time the storm ended, Venice, of course, was pretty much destroyed. But Venetians are used to that; Venice gets pretty much destroyed every decade or two.

Everyone just digs in and digs out and stays busy. The gondoliers set about replacing the roof of their Church and doing their very best to get the tubby place back to its former shape. Since it wasn't a building of great splendor to begin with, they were done in a month.

The rest of the city took longer, but by the time the tourists started returning, Venice was coming along. And by the time the rich tourists returned, in May, it was as if the Killer Storm had happened to Palermo or some other place.

Of all the rich tourists, the richest was the Queen of Corsica, who spent the entire month with her staff of maids and butlers on the whole top floor of the Gritti Palace Hotel. Not only did she bring them all with her, she hired George of the Gritti personally to take her wherever she wanted to go, twenty-four hours a day.

On the morning of the first of May he helped her into his glittering, freshly painted black gondola, and her staff brought her a dozen or more feather pillows. When she was finally comfortable she nodded, and George pushed off into the Grand Canal.

The Queen of Corsica did what she always did then—she wiggled around until she was all but invisible inside her mountain of feathers and smiled at the perfect day and said, "Sing for me, George, start with *O Sole Mio*."

George nodded and took a breath; then he raised the finest voice in Venice in song: "*O Sole Mio—*" he began.

The Queen of Corsica almost fell off her pillows shrieking "*STOPPPPP!*"

George stopped.

"That was terrible," she said. "Are you sick?"

"I am quite well, Highness."

"Do it right this time," she commanded.

George again began *O Sole Mio.*

The Queen of Corsica had a very short temper and it had already snapped. "No jokes are ever played on me!"

George was silent.

"That's the most revolting sound I've ever heard."

"That is how I sing, Highness; now and forever."

"Well then take me right back, I'm switching gondoliers."

George took her back and she switched gondoliers. When they were underway, she asked this one to sing, but he sounded almost exactly like George—

—who, it might be added here, sounded very much like Luigi.

The Queen of Corsica tried two more gondoliers, and when the results were the same she flew, in a rage, inside the hotel and packed and went down to the Danieli and took over the top floor there.

But the gondoliers at the Danieli were no better than the ones at the Gritti. By the end of the day the news had spread across Venice: all the gondoliers sounded like Luigi now.

The Mayor of Venice called an immediate meeting with the Gondolier's Council. The Mayor had won the election by campaigning furiously on the importance of preserving the natural beauty of the city; but he also owned eleven souvenir stands along the Piazza San Marco and so had more than a little interest in tourism. "You will destroy business if this keeps up," the Mayor said. His voice grew very loud. "Why are you doing it? I demand an explanation."

Quietly, George of the Gritti replied: "We are gondoliers and we make our own decisions; explanations are not a part of our vocabulary."

"But that noise, that terrible noise you make—"

"—we prefer to think of it as 'offbeat,'" George said.

The Mayor began to sense he was in the ring against a heavyweight. "But—but must you all sound exactly like Luigi?"

"We don't quite have it down yet," George admitted. "But we're getting there."

The Mayor sagged. "The tourists will stop coming."

"The tourists will never stop coming," George told him. "If they don't like the way we sing, let them hire accordian players."

Which is what happened.

Gradually. In the next months, people would get into gondolas and request *O Sole Mio*—but the results were never pleasing to them. The requests grew fewer and fewer. Within two years, the gondoliers, as popular as ever, rowed silently through the magical canals.

And no one complained.

No one complained about Luigi either—he was a full-fledged gondolier now—no reason for washing dishes when gondoliers had but to steer their crafts.

He took his place in front of the Ignazione Hotel, and his boat always sparkled, and he drank many pitchers of beer in the Gondolier's Tavern.

Which was where he happened to meet the daughter of Porky VIII. She had been very fat as a child, but then when she reached her twenties, she slimmed beautifully—her genes were the reverse of the rest of her family. She had night-black eyes, but inside she was always bright, and even John the Bastard managed to keep his scowling to a minimum when the couple wed. And they had children, many, many—even today if you walk by the Ignazione and see a gondolier with a goony smile, you can have no doubt who his ancestors were.

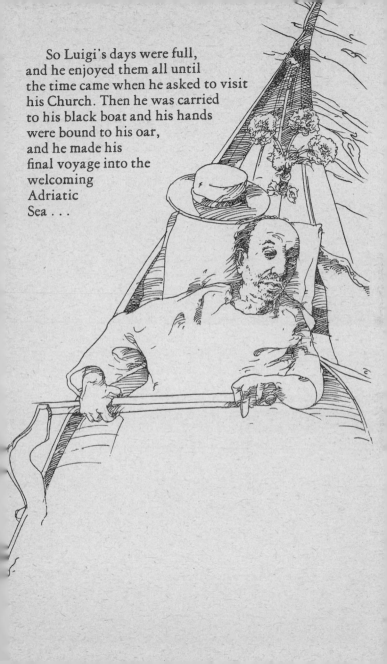

So Luigi's days were full,
and he enjoyed them all until
the time came when he asked to visit
his Church. Then he was carried
to his black boat and his hands
were bound to his oar,
and he made his
final voyage into the
welcoming
Adriatic
Sea . . .

That pretty much takes care of my research, but as always, there are basic unanswered questions. In this case, really only one basic question: the behavior of the gondoliers.

Personally, I cannot fault them—I who heard the gondoliers sing as a child and count that moment as one of the treasures of my existence. But there are those who do.

Some say the gondoliers did what they did because of fear—fear that with the coming popularity of the phonograph record, people would realize they were not such great singers, merely ordinary singers singing in a great place.

I don't believe that.

Others say the gondoliers did what they did because of boredom—after all, how often can you belt *O Sole Mio* without going crazy?

I don't believe that either.

What do I believe?

Just this: they did what they did because they had no other choice. They did it because they had to.

Why?

Because when someone special happens, he rubs off on everybody . . .

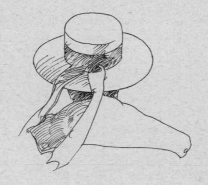

ABOUT THE AUTHOR

*Many critics of European literature
in general and Florinese prose in particular
rate S. Morgenstern as a modern master.
He is known in this country primarily for
his classic tale of true love and high adventure,*
The Princess Bride.

*Mr. Morgenstern lives in Florin City
and had, at the time of his writing this book,
one wife, two daughters,
and four and a half grandchildren.*

ABOUT THE ILLUSTRATOR

*Born in Greece, Paul Giovanopoulos came
to America in 1956. Paul is a Gold Medal
recipient from the Society of Illustrators.
His work is displayed in the permanent
collection of 24 museums. He paints and
illustrates in New York,
where he lives with his wife, Jami.*

St. Mark's Cathedral

DEL REY BOOKS

From the award-winning master of both Science Fiction and Fantasy...

PIERS ANTHONY